AdoraBULL

For Ali and Alfred, AD • For Dara and Bump, AW

Written by
Alison Donald

Illustrated by
Alex Willmore

ADORABLE

so
cute

ALFRED

BOWS

SWEET

puppy

small

SPOTS

HEARTS

maybe a
BOW?

Tom and Alfred were the best of friends.

This is Tom.

And this is Alfred.

They shared their toys, their love of the outdoors...

...and even their dreams. Alfred and Tom were inseparable until...

...Tom started school. Alfred watched and waited each day for Tom to return home.

One day after school, Tom said, "Mum, Dad, I need a pet."

"It has to be cute and snuggly and absolutely, totally..."

Alfred snorted. He didn't like the sound of this. What did adorable even mean?

He decided to find out. Alfred borrowed the farmer's phone and did a search. He saw:

kittens surrounded by marshmallows,

hamsters on tiny swings, and a puppy in a teacup.

"Ridiculous," Alfred scoffed.
But then Alfred saw something that
was so **undeniably adorable**...

...that his big bull heart softened. It was a big goat pushing a baby goat in a trolley. "Aww," Alfred sighed.

Why, he could do that! Then Tom wouldn't need to get a pet.
He nudged a baby calf into a wheelbarrow and pushed him
around the farm... but not everyone was impressed.

"Alfred!" shouted the farmer, "What is all this mess?"

This was going to be harder than he thought.

If he wanted to look truly adorable, he was going to need a new look. Alfred visited a hair salon.

He strutted home and waited for the barn animals to swoon and sigh at his adorableness. But instead...

...they laughed. And so did Tom.
"Let's clean you up Alfred, you look silly," Tom said.

Alfred sighed. He was running out of ideas. He scratched his head and remembered the pictures on the farmer's phone.

If a hamster on a swing is adorable then why not...

...a BULL?

Alfred hung his head. Bulls are reliable, and dependable, but never adorable. Alfred needed to be alone. Just as night was closing in, Alfred heard footsteps.

It was Tom. "I've been looking everywhere for you, Alfred." "Here," said Tom. "For you." Alfred couldn't believe his eyes. It was a tiny...

...kitten.

"Now you won't be so lonely when I'm at school," said Tom.

Alfred looked at the kitten and
his big bull heart melted.

That night, Alfred cared for his new kitten.
And without even trying, they were...

...absolutely, totally, undeniably

ADORABLE.

The End.

ADORABLE

so cute

ALFRED

BOWS

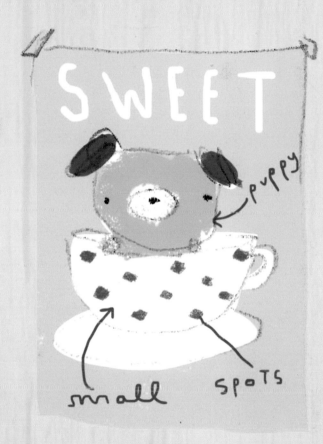

SWEET

puppy

small

SPOTS

HEARTS

maybe a BOW?

AdoraBULL

An original concept by author Alison Donald

© Alison Donald

Illustrated by Alex Willmore

© Alex Willmore

MAVERICK ARTS PUBLISHING LTD

Studio 3A, City Business Centre, 6 Brighton Road, Horsham, West Sussex, RH13 5BB

© Maverick Arts Publishing Limited   +44 (0)1403 256941

Published March 2018

A CIP catalogue record for this book is available at the British Library.

ISBN 978-1-84886-322-4

Maverick
arts publishing
www.maverickbooks.co.uk